Jaded
The Surrender Club Series
by
Reba Bale

Copyright

About This Book

They say love can find you anywhere, but this was the last place they expected to find each other!

Lauren has been initiating new submissives at the Surrender Club for many years, but lately it's all become...boring. She's jaded, ready to hang up her paddle and spend some time at home. Until she sees the new bartender...

Kristina has always longed to explore her secret fantasies, but now that she's working at the nation's premier women only BDSM club, she can see what it's really like to submit to someone. When her boss matches her with Mistress Lauren for her first-ever play session, she can't say no. There's something about the sexy and dominant older woman that makes her want to spend time with her. Maybe forever.

When a spanking turns into much, much more these two women are forced to admit that sometimes love at first sight actually happens in real life.

Jaded is book one in the *Surrender Club* instalove lesbian romance series. Each book is a fun and steamy standalone with matchmaking dommes, loving relationships, and a sweet happily ever after.

These books are intended for mature audiences.

Be sure to check out a free preview of Reba Bale's lesbian romance "The Divorcee's First Time" at the end of this book!

Dedication

This book is dedicated to everyone who's ever read a spanking romance book and thought, "I wouldn't mind meeting that sexy pirate".

Join My Newsletter

Want a free book? Join my weekly newsletter and you'll receive a fun subscriber gift. I promise I will only email you when there are new releases, free books, or special sales you'll want to see.

Visit my newsletter sign-up page at bit.ly/RebaBaleSapphic[1] to join today.

Lauren

"Have you been tied up before?"

The submissive's eyes widened with a combination of interest and fear. I resisted the urge to roll my own eyes. Newbies were so exhausting.

I didn't used to feel this way. I used to love it when I'd come to the Surrender Club and be matched up with some fresh young woman. I loved being the first one to mar their perfect skin with my palm or my paddle. I loved watching them yield to me and embrace their newly discovered submissive side.

Now, every woman who walked through the door seemed the same. They were all in their twenties, straight, and looking to explore their fantasies with someone they knew wouldn't hurt them. Too much. The newbies always thought I'd go easier on them than a male dom. They were always wrong.

I hadn't even bothered to get this one's name. She was average height, average weight, with hair darker than blonde but lighter than brown. Her breasts were way too small for my taste, but she had a decent ass, round and pale. It would be red soon.

These sessions weren't about sex anyway. At least not for me.

"Tied up?" The sub seemed confused by my question. "No."

I grabbed her chin, squeezing it tight. "You will address me as Mistress."

"Yes ma'am. I mean Mistress."

She fidgeted in the submissive posture I'd put her in: on her knees with her ass resting on her heels, palms facing up on her thighs, head down. Well, it was down until she answered my question.

"Keep your eyes on the floor," I growled, making my tone as menacing as posble.

She jumped. "Yes, Mistress ma'am."

This time I didn't resist the eye roll. I hadn't really wanted to come to Surrender tonight. It had been a long week and I didn't have the energy for the monthly "first timers" night. In my day job I was a contract attorney, and nothing sucked the life out of a person faster than a long week of staring at legalese hoping to find a loophole for an angry client.

Honestly, I didn't like my job that much, but it paid the bills. Until the last year, playing at Surrender filled my need for excitement.

I hadn't been coming to the club as much lately, but yesterday Angela, the club's owner, had reached out to me, tempting me with the promise of a month's free membership if I scened with some of the guests. Honestly, I'd been toying with the idea of quitting the club altogether. But it was exorbitantly expensive to belong to this exclusive club, so I'd be an idiot to turn down the offer of a free month.

Several of our regular dommes had gotten into committed relationships over the last few months, and while you didn't have to have sex to scene with someone – in fact, I rarely did – I understood how people's partners would feel uncomfortable about their girlfriend spending the night with her fingers in some other woman's pussy.

It would be a woman too. People who identified as male were not allowed at the Surrender Club. Angela wanted this to be a safe place for women. You didn't need to be a lesbian to come here, but you definitely needed a vagina.

I eyed my wanna-be submissive carefully. Based on her inability to sit still, I knew she was going to be a wiggler. I didn't have the patience for a wiggler, not after dealing with the other wiggling newbie before her. I definitely needed to restrain this one before I gave her the spanking that she'd come for.

"Stand up," I ordered.

She popped up to her feet with the easy grace of a woman with knees that were less than thirty years old.

I reached out to grab the strip of bare skin at her waist. She was wearing a tight miniskirt, knee high leather boots, and a corset, no doubt assuming this was what a person wore to a BDSM club. In fairness, it often was. Using my finger nails, I pinched her. Hard. She squealed.

"When I address you, you will respond to me. Do you understand me, girl?"

"Yes ma'am, Mistress."

I smothered a sigh.

"Lay face down on that bench."

I grabbed some velcro restraints from one of the drawers built into the wall. I didn't like to use handcuffs on the first timers. I made quick work of restraining her ankles and hands then brought my palm down on her milky white ass, ignoring her cry of surprise. The sooner I reddened this girl's ass, the sooner I could go home and have a glass of wine.

***

"How was it?"

Angela Lewis was stunning. Tall, curvy, and commanding. She had a smooth face and a head of dark silver hair, the juxtaposition making it difficult to place her age. She could be forty, she could be sixty, no one knew. What we did know is that she had turned Surrender into the premiere BDSM club in the region, her focus on serving only woman heightening her success. A lot of women avoided the other clubs due to fears of assholes masquerading as alphas.

The club might have catered to the softer side of BDSM, but Angela still ran a tight ship. No one got away with any bad behavior here. Like most regulars here, I was half in love with Angela and half afraid of her.

"Eh. It was fine. She was crying from the beginning. Working through some trauma I'm betting. She hit subspace pretty fast, so I stayed with her through aftercare until I knew she was okay to go. She seemed happy and alert when she left with her friend."

Angela nodded. "Well, thanks for coming in tonight, I appreciate it. The club's been busy lately and I hate to turn away business."

"No problem," I lied.

She looked up at the approaching bartender. "First drink is on the house for Mistress Lauren please, Kristina."

My breath caught as I got a look at a staff member who I'd never seen before.

"Are you new here?"

My voice was harsher than I intended but Kristina still met my gaze. It was like looking into the sun. The woman was beautiful.

She was maybe ten years younger than me, early thirties by my estimate. Long, dark hair hung straight down to her shoulders, a fringe of bangs bracketing her large brown eyes. She lowered her eyes briefly, looking almost confused, then looked back up at me.

Kristina was clearly submissive. I had a flash of her on her knees, hands tied behind her back, while she licked my pussy. Arousal hit me in a wave as every nerve in my body fired into action at once.

"Yes, Mistress, it's my second week here."

Her voice was clear but appropriately deferential. The club had a strict hierarchy and even the staff adhered to it. At least while we were inside the club.

I reached out to shake her hand, desperate to touch her. "Hi Kristina, I'm Mistress Lauren. Welcome to Surrender."

I saw a flash of surprise cross her pale face as our skin touched. Good, she felt it too, that little jolt of electricity or whatever it was that made my palm tingle. I held onto her fingers a little longer than I needed to. When Kristina pulled back, I saw her subtly wipe her palm on her thigh as she lowered her gaze back to the floor, worrying her lower lip with her teeth.

Angela's gaze was speculative as she looked between us.

"You know Lauren, Kristina has shared with me that she'd like to scene with someone. See what we offer here. And she's off in...," she glanced up at the clock behind the bar, "ten minutes. I think you're the perfect domme to initiate her into the lifestyle if you're up for another round tonight."

Kristina

I looked into Lauren's beautiful brown eyes for a long moment before I realized that I wasn't supposed to make eye contact with the dommes. I was new to this club and new to real life BDSM. Playing with people online and reading books wasn't the same, not at all.

Nothing in a book prepared me for the raw power I felt coming from Mistress Lauren. Or the desire to drop to my knees and beg her to let me service her. I hadn't had this reaction to any of the other dommes at the club though. It was something about Lauren in particular that made me feel...tingly.

The woman was stunning. I'd noticed her the second she'd come into the club earlier tonight. She was older than me, maybe late thirties or early forties with a lean but curvy body. The domme was average height, maybe five-four or five-five without her heels, and she had tousled blonde hair and thick, pouty lips that were painted a dark red.

She was wearing a short black dress that fit her like a second skin. When she turned around to respond to someone's greeting, I realized it was completely backless, cut down all the way to the upper curve of her ass. I damn near swallowed my tongue at that expanse of smooth skin.

I'd always been bi-curious, and I'd fooled around with a couple of women in the past, but somehow all my sexual partners had been men. Maybe because I'd never met someone like Lauren before. I had the oddest feeling that she was who I'd been waiting a lifetime for.

"Do you want to scene, little girl?"

I pressed my thighs together, the diminutive turning me on even when it shouldn't. I was thirty-two, far from a little girl. All this focused attention from the dominant and stunningly beautiful woman was making me giddy.

"Yes, Mistress."

My boss Angela consulted the iPad that seemed permanently attached to her hand.

"Room seven is open for the hour."

I knew from working here that room seven was one of the all-purpose playrooms, adaptable to most scenes.

"I guess I'll have to wait on that drink," Lauren said.

The club didn't allow drinking before scenes. She grabbed a bottle of water from the tray on the bar top.

"I'll meet you there. Don't dawdle."

I watched her walk away, my eyes fixed on her bare back. I was simultaneously excited and nervous. Excited that I was about to try my first scene, and nervous because I had a feeling that meeting Lauren was going to change everything.

When my shift ended, I cashed out my register and went to the employee locker room to freshen up and stash my tips in my purse. That was one of the perks of working here, the tips were great. Much better than any other club where I'd bartended. Although this wasn't like any other club.

I stopped to pee and wash my face, then headed down the hallway leading to the private playrooms. The Surrender Club was a huge space with a dance floor, various play stations, and several private rooms. You could dance while watching someone get a whipping at a St. Andrew's Cross, sit in the lounge area with a sub over your knee, enjoy one of the themed playrooms, or do something private.

I was glad Lauren chose a private room. I didn't know how I'd react to a real life BDSM scenario, and I really didn't want an audience of my new coworkers. Plus, I was dying to be alone with her.

This isn't a date, I reminded myself. *Just because you have a crush on Lauren, it doesn't mean you should be a weirdo.*

Lauren was standing in the corner of the room when I entered. I saw her take a deep breath, and then she donned her domme persona. It was fascinating to watch, almost like she'd flipped a switch. She'd exuded a friendly warmth at the bar, but in here, she was cold and detached.

"Angela gave me your paperwork," she started.

"My paperwork, Mistress?"

"With your likes, dislikes, hard limits."

I nodded, remembering that Angela had asked that any staff who wished to play after hours fill out the standard intake paperwork that the customers completed. We'd also had a thorough background check that rivaled the FBI's.

"Oh yes, thank you, Mistress."

She glanced at her phone where she presumably was reviewing my intake form.

"It says you've never been spanked, but you want to be. Any impact play including with implements is acceptable. Sex – oral, vaginal, or anal – is okay too. No blood play, scat, urine, gagging, or sensory deprivation."

"Yes, Mistress."

I'd read enough books and spent enough time on the BDSM forums to understand how to address Lauren while we scened.

"Is a blindfold okay?"

"Yes, Mistress."

"Very well. Take off all your clothes and assume the position."

I pulled off my tank top and skirt, then kicked off my shoes, leaving myself in just panties and a bra. When I hesitated, Lauren barked, "now!"

Normally I didn't like people ordering me around, but with Lauren, I didn't mind. I removed my bra and stepped out of my panties, wishing I'd worn something cuter today. Then again, I didn't know anyone else was going to see them besides me.

I lowered to the floor, dropping my ass to my heels, and placed my hands on my thighs. My gaze was fixed to the floor, but from the corner of my eye I could see Lauren move closer to me.

I couldn't help but wonder if she liked what she saw. I was curvier than some of the other subs who came to the club, but then again I was also a little older. Even though I took good care of myself, it was still hard to fight gravity. And being on display like this, totally naked while the other person was clothed, was definitely a little weird.

Lauren moved behind me and tapped lightly between my shoulder blades.

"Straighten your spine and show me those tits."

I adjusted my posture and drew my shoulder blades closer together, the movement bringing my heavy breasts into prominence. I risked a glance up at Lauren from beneath my lashes and saw her gaze pinned to my breasts. My nipples tightened in excitement.

"Good girl."

Warmth flooded my core at her praise.

Lauren walked around me slowly, her sharp gaze examining every inch of my body. She walked away, then returned with what looked like a silk scarf.

"I won't blindfold you this first time, but I will restrain you."

I thrilled at her insinuation that we'd do this again. And then I cried out.

Lauren

I couldn't resist giving those perky tits a firm pinch to punish Kristina for not responding. I took one in each hand, pressing my fingers together while pulling her nipples outward at the same time. Kristina made a yelping noise that soothed the sadist inside me.

"You will answer me when I speak to you, girl."

"Yes, Mistress," she gasped.

I released her nipples.

"Stand up."

"Yes, Mistress."

I walked around her, tying her hands loosely at the small of her back, just enough to give her the feeling of being restrained. I ran my hands down her spine like I was counting her vertebrae, then squeezed the luscious globes of her ass. I couldn't wait to mark her. Stepping closer, close enough that my front was only an inch or two from her back, I whispered in her ear.

"If you're a good girl – a very good girl – I'll let you come."

She shuddered, a delightful pink rising up her cheeks. She liked the idea. Good, so did I. I rarely cared enough to get my girls off anymore, but there was no way Kristina would be leaving this room without being satisfied.

"And if I'm a bad girl, Mistress?"

Her voice was teasing, and god help me, I loved that bratty side.

"You won't be able to sit tomorrow."

I stepped back and gave her ass a hard slap for emphasis. She jumped, and I smacked her again.

"Over the bench. Face down."

"Yes, Mistress."

I couldn't help but contrast my feelings earlier against now. Putting the last two girls I'd scened with tonight over the bench had been rote, a fast and easy way to give the newbie a safe taste of submission. Putting Kristina over it felt hot as fuck. I was regretting that I hadn't started with her over my knee.

Being with her in here felt like the beginning of something. I only hoped I wasn't just imagining the intense connection between us. It wasn't like me to so immediately into someone. I was normally guarded with my emotions.

She walked over to the bench, gracefully kneeling on the pads and laying her upper body on the cushion without assistance, seemingly untroubled by having her hands bound behind her. Even though it was her first time, she seemed to know what she was doing.

I ran my hand down her spine again. "What's your safe word?"

"Red, Mistress."

The club usually used the red, yellow, and green stoplight system unless a sub preferred to use a different safe word. I always checked to make sure there'd be no misunderstandings.

After stroking the softness of her ass a few times, I brought my hand down hard, the slap of my palm against her skin loud in the soundproofed room.

Thwack!

She jumped but didn't make a sound. The next time I brought my hand down, I covered her other cheek. Her flesh jiggled beneath my palm.

Thwack!

Noting with satisfaction that she already was turning a little pink, I began spanking her with a steady rhythm.

Thwack!

Thwack!

I didn't speak, focused on my task. Kristina was silent other than the increasing harshness of her breath as the pain increased. I spanked her briskly, moving my hand from side to side until the entirety of her ass was nicely red.

I wanted it redder though. Needed it.

"Stay."

"Yes, Mistress."

Her voice still sounded strong and steady. I strode over to the implement closet, returning with a small leather paddle. It was black, about three or four inches wide with a long handle that allowed greater control of my strikes. It was one of my favorite tools.

"Where are you right now?"

Understanding my question immediately, Kristina answered, "Green, Mistress."

"Good girl."

She cried out for the first time as the leather cracked across her skin. I smiled as I struck her again. My body moved automatically, categorizing her reactions, adjusting my swings, noticing the moment when she started lifting her ass to meet the paddle.

My little sub liked being spanked. I was betting that her pussy was already wet. I took a break from spanking her to confirm that suspicion, my mouth quirking up with satisfaction as I encountered her cream.

"This arouses you."

"Yes, Mistress."

There wasn't a trace of embarrassment in her voice. Not that there should be. People liked spanking for a variety of reasons. It was cathartic. It calmed the mind. And for many, it helped fulfil their sexual fantasies.

I wondered what other fantasies Kristina had. I was looking forward to trying them all with her.

I resumed spanking her with the leather paddle, avoiding hitting her in the same place twice in a row. After all these years in the lifestyle, I could practically do this with my eyes closed. But I also knew that it was important to pay close attention. As my submissive, at least for this hour, Kristina's health and welfare needed to be my top priority.

That didn't stop me from analyzing why this woman was affecting me so much. We hadn't even had a proper conversation and I knew I could never let her go. I just hoped she felt the same.

"Ahh!"

I stepped back, realizing that my paddle had broached the lowest curve of her ass, leaving a mark across the top of her thigh. Her skin was a bright red color now, and I knew it would be throbbing with heat. I dropped the paddle and went to find the arnica cream. Kristina's hands were still behind her back, so I untied the ribbon.

"Stretch your arms out and hang them towards the floor for a few minutes to get the circulation going again."

"Yes, Mistress."

Her voice sounded dream-like, telling me she was floating. We hadn't done enough to get her to subspace – especially because she clearly liked pain – but she was definitely feeling good right now. Kristina had taken to submission like a natural.

As I rubbed the soothing salve on her skin I asked, "You haven't done this before? None of your partners have spanked you?"

"No, Mistress. I tried to ask a few times, but no one was up for it."

Damn vanillas. They didn't understand that there was a wide range between boring missionary sex and being hog-tied and whipped. I'd known quite a few people who'd thought a simple spanking was the on-ramp to torture and abuse.

"But you've studied? Usually when I scene with someone for the first time, they need more explicit instructions."

"I've read a lot of books and played in online forums, Mistress. I just, um, never found anyone in real life to learn from."

"Where are you now, girl?"

"Green, Mistress."

"Can you take more?"

"Yes, Mistress."

"Good girl. Get on your knees."

Kristina

I'd dreamed of being spanked for so long I could hardly believe any of this was real.

When I was twelve years old, I'd snuck one of my mother's romance books out of her bedroom. *The Pirate's Prize* was about a handsome but stern pirate who discovers a stowaway on his ship. The young woman ran away, intending to escape her wicked stepmother, but the pirate has no time for excuses. He puts her over his knee and spanks her until she's begging for forgiveness, and then he kisses her, and she discovers the heady combination of pain and pleasure. Then they lived happily ever after.

I'd read every spanking romance I could get my hands on ever since.

I wanted to experience pain. Loss of control. The emptying of my mind. Surrender.

I didn't like the hard stuff. I wanted to be spanked, not whipped. Called a slut, not peed on. I wanted a hand around my neck, but not to be choked out. I craved the kind of pain that brings you right to the edge, that heightens arousal and makes everything more intense.

Over the years, I'd hinted around with a few of my lovers that I'd like to have things get a little rougher in the bedroom, but they'd acted like I was crazy. One guy had told me I should get therapy for whatever abuse I'd suffered as a child, as if that's the only reason a person might want to be spanked.

That's why I'd jumped at the chance to work at Surrender. Besides the fact that it paid very well, all staff got free membership to the club, and we were free to play any time after working hours.

This job was my chance to finally try BDSM. But I didn't expect to find her. Mistress Lauren. I was already obsessed with her, and when she ordered me to my knees I didn't hesitate to comply.

I kept my eyes down until Lauren squatted in front of me. The movement made her short skirt hike up her thighs, revealing a triangle of lace. I was so fixated on that view that I didn't notice what the domme was doing until she grabbed my nipple and pulled hard. I glanced up to see her affixing a clamp to my left breast.

I hissed in a breath. Nipple clamps. Something else I'd always wanted to try. The pain was exquisite, making my entire torso hum.

Lauren made quick work of clamping the other nipple. The clamps were connected by a thin chain. When she shifted the chain, it added more pressure to the clamps. I bit my lip and tried to breathe through the intense pain.

"Good girl," she whispered.

I couldn't help but smile. Apparently, I was a praise slut. I'd had no idea.

"Have you ever licked a pussy?"

"No, Mistress."

I'd never gone down on a woman before, but right now I wanted it more than I'd ever wanted anything in my life. Lauren's eyes flared with what looked like interest. Or maybe satisfaction. She wanted me to give her pleasure as much as I wanted to give it to her.

"You have pleased me, so as a reward I will let you eat me out until I come," she told me. "And then you will lick me clean."

"Yes, Mistress."

She walked to the other side of the room and leaned her back against a clear expanse of wall. Her lithe figure stood in contrast to the bright white paint. The entire room was bright and modern looking, not at all the dark dingy dungeon feel I'd expected when I started working here.

Lauren crooked her finger at me.

"Come."

"Yes, Mistress."

I started to push to my feet, but she held up one hand.

"You will crawl. On your hands and knees like a good pet."

I was already wet, but that stark order made my pussy gush. I pressed my thighs together for an instant and then dropped to hands and knees, crying out when the movement caused the clamps to pull uncomfortably on my nipples. They were already turning a dark red, engorged and angry.

I crawled across the room, my face red with humiliation at being ordered to crawl. I moved slowly and carefully, vainly trying to minimize the sway of my breasts. I wondered if this was easier for girls who weren't D cups. By the time I reached Lauren I was panting from the pain, my breasts feeling like they were on fire. When I automatically shifted up to the submissive position, she patted my head like I was a dog.

"Good girl."

I glowed under her praise.

Lauren rolled her dress up to her waist, revealing her black lace panties. My mouth watered.

"Take them off with your teeth."

"Yes, Mistress."

Eagerly I scooted forward and caught her waistband in my teeth. The fabric got caught on the curve of her ass, but I didn't dare disobey the order to use only my teeth. I tugged and maneuvered until Lauren helped me out by sliding the fabric past her ass. When I'd gotten her panties to her ankles, she lifted one foot and then the other, and I helped her step out of them altogether.

I sat back up, still holding her panties in my teeth, and her eyes twinkled with amusement.

"I would gag you with those if I didn't need you to use your mouth. You may set them down."

Shuffling forward, I awaited further instructions while I gazed with interest at her pussy. It was bare other than a patch of dark blonde hair at her apex, the pink folds glistening in the light. I licked my lips, desperate to get a taste of her.

"You may begin."

"Yes, Mistress," I said, not even caring how eager my voice sounded.

I licked her right up the center, then did it a second time, sliding my tongue between her lower lips. She tasted delicious. Emboldened, I used my hands to open her up wider and started eating her out with an enthusiasm that I only hoped would cover my lack of experience. The domme hummed her approval.

"Add your fingers," Lauren instructed after a couple of minutes. "First one, then a second one. Fuck me with your hand."

"Yes, Mistress," I mumbled against her pussy.

Tentatively, I slid my pointer finger inside her channel, pumping in and out a few times before adding a second one. When I heard Lauren's breath quicken I knew I was on the right track. I increased the speed of my thrusts and started circling her clit with my tongue at the same time.

"Kristina!"

It was the first time since we'd entered the playroom that Lauren used my name. I hummed against her clit, adding a little bit of suction.

"Yes, there, like that."

Lauren's hand tunneled into my hair, pulling the strands painfully as she ground her pussy against my face. The excitement of bringing her pleasure, combined with the pain from the nipple clamps and the pulling on my hair all combined to bring me dangerously close to an orgasm. I pressed my thighs together.

Somehow, she noticed.

"You can't come without permission," she rasped. Her voice had turned from firm and cold to soft and breathless, letting me know she must be close to release.

It only took a few more minutes before she gasped, "God!" and then I felt a rush of moisture against my fingers as Lauren started to come.

I looked up to see her back arched against the wall, her body shaking. Her eyes were closed, and her face was screwed up in a look that could only be described as ecstasy. I loved that I'd brought her pleasure. I loved that I'd made her lose control, just a little bit.

Lauren pushed at my head, and I pulled away, sitting back on my heels again. My fingers were dripping with her cum, and I couldn't resist bringing them to my mouth for another taste of her. I looked up at her from beneath my lashes as I did it.

"Oh, you are a dirty little girl, aren't you?" Lauren said, approval in her voice. Her body was still shaking from her intense orgasm.

"Yes, Mistress," I answered politely.

"Well, you've earned a reward nonetheless. I haven't come that hard in a long time. Maybe ever. Stand up please."

When I got to my feet she grabbed my shoulders, turning us so my back was against the wall now. Our eyes met and maybe I was crazy, but I could swear I saw real emotion there. Something that looked a lot like passion. Before I could analyze it, Lauren's mouth crushed against mine.

Somewhere in the back of my mind I remembered that there was no kissing during scenes, not unless the couple was, well, a couple. I supposed it happened sometimes, but in general kissing was an intimacy reserved for long-term partners. I wondered what it meant that Lauren was kissing me.

Lauren bit down on my bottom lip hard enough to sting and I opened for her. Her tongue swooped in, dominating my mouth the same way she'd dominated the rest of my body. I moaned deep in my throat and slid my tongue against hers, rocking my pelvis against hers.

We kissed for what felt like hours before she slid her hands down between us. I'd forgotten all about the nipple clamps until she pulled them both off simultaneously. I howled in pain as the blood came rushing back to my aggrieved nipples.

"Fuck!" I gasped. "That hurts."

"Did I invite you to speak?" she asked.

"No Mistress, I apologize."

I'd almost forgotten we were doing a scene. I lowered my gaze obediently, properly chastised. I breathed deeply as the pain subsided, leaving me even more aroused.

"I suppose I'll overlook it. This time." Her words were stern, but amusement danced in her eyes. "Now how about a little treat?"

Lauren

I could not wait to get my tongue on this woman. She was all lush curves and so sweetly submissive. But it was more than that. Something about her drew me in. I had the most ridiculous urge to bring her home with me. Hell, I'd even kissed her. I did not kiss people I scened with. Ever.

Kissing her had been like coming home. I wanted to do it every day for the rest of my life.

"On the couch," I ordered, making my voice colder as I reminded myself that we were still doing a scene.

I pointed at the fake leather couch in the corner. I'm sure that Angela would have sprung for real leather, but in a place like this, it was important to have furniture that could be easily cleaned between sessions.

"Yes, Mistress."

Maybe it was my imagination, but I could swear that Kristina added a little wiggle to her step. I smacked her ass with my palm, just in case. It was still red from her earlier spanking, but the color was already fading.

She stopped in front of the couch, waiting for instructions like a good submissive. I couldn't believe this was her first scene and I'd only had to correct her once. I'd corrected both of the girls I'd scened with earlier at least half a dozen times.

"On your back."

Kristina lay across the couch, her legs parted slightly. My eyes went right to her pussy, and for a second, I lost my train of thought. Her body was lush and curvy. And mine. She just didn't know it yet.

I crawled over her, laying my body on top of her like a blanket, pinning her down on the couch. Grabbing her hands, I pushed them over her head and pressed them against the arm of the couch. Her brown eyes widened with excitement.

"Leave them right there, or you won't get to come."

"Yes, Mistress."

I gave her a quick kiss, then licked my way down her neck until I reached her breasts. I knew her nipples had to be sore from the clamps, but I couldn't resist easing them a little. I closed my lips around one and Kristina arched her back, silently willing me to take more, but kept her hands up as instructed. I teased the tip with my tongue, adding just enough suction to keep her attention.

After I'd had my fill of both breasts, I kissed my way down her body, occasionally giving her more little bites to keep her guessing.

When I reached her pussy, I pushed one of her legs up onto the back of the couch and shifted the other onto the floor, opening her wide. I studied her pussy like it was a map.

Kristina was dripping wet. I gave her clit a sharp smack, making her cry out.

"I think you enjoyed your punishment a little too much, little girl. Maybe I went too easy on you."

"It was going down on you, Mistress," she said quietly, meeting my gaze. "It turned me on. A lot."

Her answer thrilled me. I'd be dreaming about that orgasm she gave me for a long time. Hopefully it was the first of many.

"Have you ever been with a woman before?" I asked curiously.

She had seemed tentative at first, almost like she was learning as she went along, but then her movements had grown bolder. I didn't normally ask the people I played with personal questions, but with this woman, I wanted to know everything.

I leaned down and bit the sensitive skin of her inner thigh while I waited for an answer.

"I've kissed women before," she answered breathlessly. "And one time a woman touched my breasts. But I've never had sex with a woman, Mistress."

"Good."

I felt a primal sense of satisfaction knowing that I'd be the first woman to touch this sweet little pussy, although I didn't want to analyze that too closely. I cupped it with my hand, giving it a little squeeze.

"I'm going to play with your pussy, but you can't come until I give you permission, do you understand?"

"Yes, Mistress."

I began with my hand, stroking the pads of my fingers over the external part of her pussy. She was smooth and soft. Slowly I slid one finger in between her labia, stroking up and down the length of her channel over and over again, spreading her moisture. She moaned softly, her hips punching up to get closer.

After teasing her for a few minutes, I scooted down between her legs. Lowering my head, I followed the same trail with my tongue, licking her firmly from right above her asshole to her clit. She tasted sweet and tangy. She tasted like mine.

Tilting my head, I sucked one of her labia into my mouth – at least as much as I could get in there – and closed my jaw, pinching her gently. She shuddered. I kissed my way up to her apex, then repeated my gentle bite on the other side.

When I couldn't take it anymore, I slid my tongue into her opening and began fucking her with it. My pussy was gushing, despite my recent orgasm.

Kristina rocked her hips urgently against my face. When I looked up from between her legs, her eyes were closed, and her lips were rolled in like she was trying to keep from crying out. Her hands were still pressed firmly against the arm of the couch.

I renewed my efforts, roughly sliding my tongue in and out until she was quivering with need.

"Don't come yet," I reminded her.

"Yes, Mistress."

Someday I'd edge this woman for hours. Until she was sobbing with need and begging to come. But we didn't have a lot of time left in the playroom, and I wanted to see her come more than I wanted to take my next breath.

I licked up her channel and began tapping at her clit with the tip of my tongue. Her fingers flexed against the couch arm, and she made the sweetest little whimpering noises as she struggled to maintain control.

I slid my finger into her opening, and then a second one, scissoring my fingers apart to stretch her opening. Her breath stuttered in her chest as I began finger fucking her with rough strokes while I continued to tease her clit.

Her inner muscles seized, telling me she was close again, and I removed my fingers. She made a soft sound of frustration, and I slapped her clit sharply, making her cry out.

"Do you want to come now, girl?"

"Yes, Mistress."

Her face was flushed, her body trembling against the couch.

"Beg me."

I loved it when they begged. Kristina winced, but I felt another flood of moisture against the fingers that cupped her mound. She seemed to like a little bit of humiliation.

"Please, Mistress. Please let me come. I'm so close."

Our eyes met, hers glassy with arousal. Her beautiful face was flushed, her expression almost desperate.

"You may come when you're ready," I told her.

Then I shoved my fingers back into her opening and slid them against her G spot while I licked her clit. Kristina let out a shrill scream as she succumbed to her orgasm.

"Oh my God," she mumbled. "Oh my God."

Her body began shaking and her back arched, those lovely tits bouncing from the motion. Her leg banged against the couch while the foot on the floor scrambled for purchase. And through it all, she kept her hands above her head.

When she finally sagged against the couch, totally spent, I removed my fingers with something that felt like regret. Placing a quick kiss on her mound, stood up, and moved her hands back down from over her head. I felt a sense of regret that we couldn't cuddle, which was weird because I'd never been a cuddler.

"You look beautiful when you come, Kristina," I whispered, leaning down to press my lips against hers one last time.

"We should get dressed," I said regretfully. "They'll need the room soon."

Kristina still looked dazed. "Oh. Um. Okay. I mean, yes Mistress."

Right on time, I heard a discreet tap on the door, letting us know that our hour was up. The noise seemed to break the spell between us, Kristina's face clearing immediately as she came back to herself. She walked slowly to the corner where she'd left her clothes, turning her back on me as she got dressed again.

I slid my dress over my head then hunted around for my panties, trying not to feel too despondent at the obvious change in atmosphere. My time with Kristina was over. I wasn't sure what I'd expected but seeing her avoid my gaze and hide from me told me she must not feel the same way I did. I'd done my job and fulfilled one of her submissive fantasies, and now she was done with me.

It figured that the one time I let myself feel something for a submissive she wasn't interested. But I was still her domme, at least for a couple more minutes and I had an obligation to take care of her.

"How are you feeling, Kristina?"

"I feel fine. Good. Thank you, Mistress."

Her tone was cool, and her gaze was fixed on the floor. I felt desperate to know what she was thinking right now.

"Look at me," I instructed.

She complied, her face a blank mask.

"Do you need instructions for how to care for yourself tonight?"

"No. I, uh, I know what to do, and I didn't drop into subspace. I feel perfectly lucid."

I studied her face, wanting to confirm what she was saying. She seemed perfectly fine, just distracted.

"And how did you like your first scene?"

"Permission to speak freely, Mistress?"

Oh God, was she going to tell me that she didn't like it? She seemed to like it but what did I really know about this woman anyway? Maybe she was a really good actress.

"Of course, our scene is officially over now. I will not punish you for anything you say."

"The scene was good. Better than I could imagine. I've never come that hard in my life. I feel both relaxed and energized, you know?"

I nearly sagged with relief that I hadn't misread her.

"Yes, that's a very common reaction."

Silence stretched between us, as if we were suddenly uncomfortable around each other. Kristina cleared her throat, looking both vulnerable and hopeful.

"I'd like to see you again, Mistress."

"You'd like to do another scene with me?" I clarified, trying to not get my hopes up.

She shook her head.

"No. I mean yes, I would like to do another scene with you," she said haltingly. "But I'd also like to see you outside the club, because the thing is, and I know this is completely crazy, but I think I've fallen in love with you."

Kristina

The second the words left my mouth I called myself an idiot. Lauren was a domme. An experienced one. She was just playing a role here.

I remembered reading about how sometimes people fell in love with their therapists, mistaking the therapeutic relationship for something more. Maybe that happened in BDSM too? Because based on Lauren's expression, what had just happened didn't mean anything to her. Not the way it did for me.

To make things worse, Lauren just stood there, staring at me in shock like she couldn't believe the words coming out of my mouth. I knew the feeling. The silence stretched between us, growing even more uncomfortable.

God, I was such an idiot, acting like a schoolgirl with a crush and putting one of our customers in an uncomfortable situation. I needed to get out of here.

I sprang for the door, taking off down the hallway towards the employee lounge. I heard Lauren call out to me, telling me to wait, which made me run harder. I slammed my badge against the scanner, slipping in the door and closing it quickly behind me.

"Kristina, wait." Lauren pounded on the locked door. "I need to talk to you."

Ignoring her, I headed out the back door, sprinting to my car that was parked in the employee lot behind the building.

Driving towards my apartment, I willed myself to take deep breaths and focus on driving safely. I debated quitting my job, then reminded myself I needed the money. Plus making a fool of myself wasn't a good reason to quit the best job I'd ever had. I'd just be casual when I saw Lauren again at the club, and we could pretend that none of this had ever happened.

This certainly wasn't the first time I'd ever embarrassed myself, and it probably wouldn't be the last. It's just that...well, nothing had ever felt so perfect before. I was usually pretty intuitive, it was one of the things that made me a good bartender, but I'd never been so wrong about someone's feelings for me.

Maybe it was just the post spanking and post orgasm endorphins speaking, but I thought there was something more between me and Lauren. Honestly, I'd kind of fell in love with her the minute I laid eyes on her.

It was ridiculous, of course. This wasn't one of those love at first sight romance books I loved to read. Lauren and I had never even had a proper conver sation. We knew absolutely nothing about each other. Well, nothing besides how each other's pussies tasted.

I didn't even know if she was single, I realized. What if I'd just hit on someone's wife or something? What had happened between us felt real and intimate and passionate, but it was clearly one sided. I was sure I'd laugh about it someday. Today wasn't that day.

Normally I took a shower before I went to bed, but I wanted to keep the scent of Lauren with me for just a little while longer, so I just threw on an old tee shirt, ate an obscene amount of ice cream, and went to bed.

When I woke again the sun was shining through my bedroom window. A quick look at my phone showed it was just after ten. I'd been a bartender for years and was used to sleeping late, but now that I was awake, I figured that I might as well get up and take a shower.

I padded into the kitchen to start the coffee maker and was on my way back to the bathroom when someone rang the doorbell. Assuming it was my neighbor, I opened it without looking.

To my shock, Lauren stood on my doorstep, looking significantly less put together than she had last night.

She was wearing faded jeans, a light blue tank top with the Surrender logo on the front, and a short black leather jacket. The hair that was carefully styled into windswept waves last night was pulled back into a stubby ponytail, and her face was completely devoid of make-up.

She looked beautiful.

"Lauren! How did...what are you doing here?"

"Can I come in?" she asked, her voice soft. "Please?"

"Sure."

What was she doing here? I hadn't had coffee yet, and there was no way I could deal with a complicated conversation this early in the morning. Maybe she was here to check on me, but she looked too subdued for that. She looked exhausted, and there were shadows under her eyes, as if she hadn't gone to bed yet.

"I was just making a pot of coffee. Do you want some?"

"Sure, that would be nice."

She followed me into the kitchen, looking around the room curiously.

"Have a seat."

Grabbing two cups from the cabinet, I pressed the pause button on the coffee pot and poured us each half a cup. We could have more when the pot was finished.

"I'm sorry but I don't have cream. I might have a packet of sugar somewhere."

"Black is fine," she answered.

I sat across from her, studying her face. She seemed so different from the confident woman I'd seen last night.

"How did you get my address?" I asked. "Did Angela give it to you?"

I hoped my boss wasn't in the habit of giving out her employee's personal information.

"No. I begged her for it repeatedly, but she wouldn't budge. She's a stickler for privacy. She told me if I wanted to see you again, I could wait for your next shift."

"Oh good."

"I didn't want to wait that long, so I did some internet stalking last night," she admitted with a wry smile. "That didn't work, so I suckered a friend who's kind of a hacker into searching for your address."

When I looked at her in shock she grimaced, looking almost embarrassed. I had a feeling it wasn't something that happened very often.

"Yeah, I know, it's a total stalker thing to do, and I apologize for the invasion of your privacy. I just, I needed to see you. To tell you something. I won't bother you again after this, if that's what you want."

I raised one eyebrow. "Go on."

"I've been coming to the club for a long time," she started. "To be honest, I've been getting tired of it. I enjoy the dynamic, creating scenes, learning how to wring the most pleasure out of someone while still bringing them to the edge of their pain threshold. But it's gotten old, to be honest. This endless parade of nameless, faceless women is exhausting."

She took a sip of her coffee, looking at me expectantly, but I didn't know what she wanted me to say.

"Why are you telling me this?"

"The thing is, I only very rarely have sex with my subs. And I never, never kiss them."

"But you kissed me," I reminded her, my lips tingling at the memory.

"Because you're different."

Unsure of how to respond to that, I took another sip of my coffee, the bitter caffeine clearing the last of the cobwebs from my brain. When I didn't respond, Lauren leaned forward, her expression turning earnest.

"When I first saw you last night, do you know what I thought?"

I shook my head.

"I thought to myself, Lauren, here you've been so jaded for so long, and now you're looking at the woman who's going to change everything."

"I don't understand."

"The thing is, I fell for you the second I saw you, Kristina. I know it sounds ridiculous, but it's true. And I've spent the entire night trying to figure out how to track you down so I could tell you."

Hope bloomed in my chest. "But last night, when I told you..."

"I know," she interrupted. "And I'm so, so sorry. I was just so shocked. I couldn't believe that you felt it too. It seemed impossible that you were having the same crazy feelings as I was. When I froze, I was thinking for a minute that maybe I wanted you to say something like that so badly that I imagined it. Like maybe I was having a hallucination."

"You didn't imagine it."

She gave me a small smile. "I know, but by the time I realized that, you were gone. You ran pretty fast for someone who I know had a sore ass."

I ran three miles every morning so that little sprint down the hallway was nothing, but this didn't seem to be the time to share that.

"So what are you saying exactly? Why are you here?"

Maybe I wanted her to work for it. Maybe I thought I was having hallucinations of my own. Either way, I wanted her to be crystal clear with her intentions.

"I want to be with you, Kristina. I want us to get to know each other better, and I want us to scene together again, and when the time is right, I want us to move in together. I know it's all way too fast, but you need to know that I want to spend the rest of our lives together. And I'm hoping to God that you feel the same."

"I'm not going to be a house slave," I shuddered. "I hate having things around my neck."

Lauren laughed. "When we are playing, I'll be your domme. But the rest of the time, we are equals. I want a partner, not a slave. I don't need to top you to get off, and I don't have the energy to be a twenty-four seven domme anyway."

I stood up and stalked around the table.

"So, since we're not at the club right now, if I were to do this, you'd be okay with it, right?"

I pulled her chair away from the table and straddled her lap, bringing my hands to either side of her face. Lauren's eyes twinkled as she waited to see what I would do. I surged forward, holding her head in place and kissing her deeply, taking control of the kiss. When Lauren kissed me back, seemingly content to let me take the lead, I knew instinctively that everything was going to be okay with us.

"How about we take this to the bedroom?" I suggested. "You can ride my face until I make you scream."

"I thought you'd never ask."

Epilogue—Lauren

Six months later...

"I'm so glad you're here tonight."

I gave Angela a smile. As usual, the club owner looked impeccable.

"I'm always glad to help train new dommes. They need to know how to do things safely." I wrapped my arm around Kristina's shoulders. "And I've got my favorite submissive to help me demonstrate."

Kristina pushed up on her toes and gave me a quick peck on the cheek. She'd really gotten into the scene, and the fact that she was willing to let me demonstrate on her beautiful body in front of an audience showed how far she'd come.

"First I need to pour some drinks."

Kristina was also on shift tonight.

It had been six months since the night we met, and we'd been blissfully happy.

After a long and intense negotiation, Kristina had moved in with me. Her lease was expiring and since I owned my house, it made sense to me. But my girl was not submissive in real life. She'd made me work hard for that cohabitation agreement. Since then, we had been spending our days off together redecorating my house to make it more ours.

I discovered that despite the difference in our ages and our disparate careers, Kristina and I had a lot in common. We both liked to cook, we liked the same TV shows, and we both had similar values around relationships. She was a little messier than I was, but we'd hired a cleaning lady to come in once a week and help out, which settled any issue we had around that.

She even had me jogging with her a few times a week now, even though I pretended to hate it. We'd met each other's families and friends, seamlessly blending our lives together. And one day, we'd think about having a baby. Or at least getting a dog.

We'd spent our first month together purposely not doing any BDSM scenes, wanting to get to know each other as equals without the power dynamics in play. We'd had sex though. Lots and lots of energetic sex.

The first night we went into a private room at Surrender to scene again, I beat her ass red for making me wait so long. The little brat had loved it. I'd realized since then that I hadn't been bored with being a domme, I'd been bored being a domme with anonymous women.

I still helped out on newbie night though. As long as I didn't have sex with the subs, Kristina was okay with it. The funny thing was that I hadn't even been able to finger another sub, let alone fuck them any other way. I was strictly a punishment domme now, and that worked out great for us. It's what most of the newbies were looking for anyway.

Kristina and I weren't the only ones who had found love at the club. Lately all the dommes had been dropping like flies, falling in love one by one, thus the interest in doing some classes to train the next group of dominants. It was always fun helping women embrace their dominant side and teaching them that you didn't have to be male to be alpha.

Even Angela was in a relationship now, and as far as any of us knew, she'd been single for over twenty years. It was fun watching my friends find the same kind of love and companionship that I enjoyed with Kristina.

"Good evening," I greeted the assembled women a while later. "My name is Mistress Lauren, and I'm here to show you how to make a woman submit."

My eyes met Kristina's across the bar.

"And maybe more."

***

You can find more of Reba's lesbian romances at
Books2read.com/rl/lesbianromance[1]
If you liked this book, please consider leaving a review or rating to let me know.
Be sure to join my newsletter for more great books. You'll receive a free book when you join my newsletter. Subscribers are the first to hear about all of my new releases and sales. Visit my mailing list sign-up at bit.ly/RebaBaleSapphic to download your free book today.

---

1. https://books2read.com/rl/lesbianromance

2. https://bit.ly/RebaBaleSapphic

Special Preview

The Divorcee's First Time
A Contemporary Lesbian Romance
By Reba Bale

"It's done," I said triumphantly. "My divorce is final."

My best friend Susan paused in the process of sliding into the restaurant booth, her sharply manicured eyebrows raising almost to her hairline. "Dickhead finally signed the papers?" she asked, her tone hopeful.

I nodded as Susan settled into the seat across from me. "The judge signed off on it today. Apparently his barely legal girlfriend is knocked up, and she wants to get a ring on her finger before the big event." I explained with a touch of irony in my voice. "The child bride finally got it done for me."

Susan smiled and nodded. "Well congratulations and good riddance. Let's order some wine."

We were most of the way through our second bottle when the conversation turned back to my ex. "I wonder if Dickhead and his Child Bride will last for the long haul," Susan mused.

I shook my head and blew a chunk of hair away from my mouth.

"I doubt it," I told her. "Someday she's gonna roll over and think, there's got to be something better out there than a self-absorbed man child who doesn't know a clitoris from a doorknob."

Susan laughed, sputtering her wine. I eyed her across the table. Although she was ten years older than me, we had been best friends for the last five years. We worked together at the accounting firm. She had been my trainer when I first came there, fresh out of school with my degree. We bonded over work, but soon realized that we were kindred spirits.

Susan was rapidly approaching forty but could easily pass for my age. Her hair was black and shiny, hinting at her Puerto Rican heritage, with blunt bangs and blond highlights that she paid a fortune for. Her face was clear and unlined, with large brown eyes and cheek bones that could cut glass. She was an avid runner and worked hard to maintain a slim physique since the women in her family ran towards the chunkier side.

I was almost her complete opposite. Blonde curls to her straight dark hair, blue eyes instead of brown, curvy where she was lean, introverted to her extrovert.

But somehow, we clicked. We were closer than sisters. Honestly, I don't know how I would have gotten through the last year without her. She had been the first one I called when my marriage fell apart, and she had supported me throughout the whole process.

It had been a big shock when I came home early one day and found my husband getting a blow job in the middle of our living room. It had been even more shocking when I saw the fresh young face at the other end of that blow job.

"What the fuck are you doing?" I had screeched, startling them both out of their sex stupor. "You're getting blow jobs from children now?"

The girl had looked up from her knees with eyes glowing in righteous indignation. "I'm not a child, I'm nineteen," she had informed me proudly. "I'm glad you finally found out. I give him what you don't, and he loves me."

I looked into the familiar eyes of my husband and saw the panic and confusion there. I made it easy for him. "Get out," I told him firmly, my voice leaving no room for argument. "Take your teenage girlfriend and get the fuck out. We're getting a divorce. Expect to hear from my lawyer."

The condo was in my name. I had purchased it before we were married, and since I had never added his name to the deed, he had no rights to it. There was no question he would be the one leaving.

My husband just stared at me with his jaw hanging open like he couldn't believe it. "But Jennifer," he whined. "You don't understand. Let me explain."

"There's nothing to understand," I told him sadly. "This is a deal breaker for me, and you know that as well as I do. We are done."

The girl had taken his hand and smiled triumphantly. "Come on baby," she told him. "Zip up and let's get out of here. We can finally be together like we planned."

"Yeah baby," I had sneered. "I'll box up your stuff. It'll be in the hallway tomorrow. Pick it up by six o'clock or I'm trashing it all."

After they left my first call was to the locksmith, but my second call was to Susan.

That night was the last time I had seen my husband until we had met for the court-ordered pre-divorce mediation. He spent most of that session reiterating what he had told me in numerous voice mails, emails and sessions spent yelling on the other side of my front door. He loved me. He had made a terrible mistake. He wasn't going to sign the papers. We were meant to be together. Needless to say, mediation hadn't been very successful. Fortunately, I had been careful to keep our assets separate, as if I knew that someday I would be in this situation.

Through it all, Susan had been my rock. In the end I don't think I was even that sad about the divorce, I was really angrier with myself for staying in a relationship that wasn't fulfilling with a man I didn't love anymore.

"You need to get some quality sex." Susan drew my attention back to the present. "Bang him out of your system."

"I don't know," I answered slowly. "I think I need a hiatus."

"A hiatus from what?" Susan asked with a frown. "You haven't had sex in what, eighteen months?"

I nodded. "Yeah, but I just can't take a disappointing fumble right now. I would rather have nothing than another three-pump chump."

I shook my head and continued, "I'm going to stick with my battery-operated boyfriend, he never disappoints me."

Susan smiled. "That's because you know your way around your own vajayjay."

She motioned to the waiter to bring us a third bottle of wine.

"That's why I like to date women," she continued. "We already know our way around the equipment."

I nodded thoughtfully. "You make a good point."

Susan leaned forward. "We've never talked about this," she said earnestly. "Have you ever been with a woman?"

For more of the story, check out "The Divorcee's First Time" by Reba Bale, available for immediate download[1] today.

***

Want a free book? Join my newsletter and a special gift. I'll contact you a few times a month with story updates, new releases, and special sales. Visit bit.ly/Re-BaleSapphic[2] for more information.

---

https://books2read.com/u/bpznKX

Other Books by Reba Bale

Check out my other books, available on most major online retailers now. Go to my webpage[1] at bit.ly/AuthorRebaBale to learn more.

Friends to Lovers Lesbian Romance Series

The Divorcee's First Time

My BFF's Sister

My Rockstar Assistant

My College Crush

My Fake Girlfriend

My Secret Crush

My Holiday Love

My Valentine's Gift

My Spring Fling

My Forbidden Love

Coming Out in Ten Dates

Worth Waiting For

The Surrender Club Lesbian Romance Series

Jaded

Hated

Fated

Menage Romances

Pie Promises

Tornado Warning

Summer in Paradise

Life of the Mardi

Bases Loaded

The Strangers Romance Series

Sinful Desires

Taken by Surprise

1. https://books2read.com/ap/nB2qJv/Reba-Bale

Just One Night

Hotwife Erotic Romances

Hotwife in the Woods

Hotwife on the Beach

Hotwife Under the Tree

A Hotwife's Retreat

Hot Wife Happy Life

Want a free book? Just join my newsletter at bit.ly/RebaBaleSapphic[2].
You'll be the first to hear about new releases, special sales, and free offers.

About the Author

Reba Bale writes erotic romance, lesbian romance, menage romance, & the spicy stories you want to read on a cold winter's night. When Reba is not writing she is reading the same naughty stories she likes to write.

You can also follow Reba on Medium[3] for free stories, bonus epilogues and more. You can also hear all about new releases and special sales by joining Reba's newsletter mailing list.[4]

---

3.   https://medium.com/@authorrebabale

4.   https://bit.ly/rebabooks

Don't miss out!

Visit the website below and you can sign up to receive emails whenever Reba Bale publishes a new book. There's no charge and no obligation.

https://books2read.com/r/B-A-IDTM-DOXNC

BOOKS 2 READ

Connecting independent readers to independent writers.

Printed in Great Britain
by Amazon

58322686R00030